AN...
THE FIRST BEAST

# BY ADAM BLADE

ORCHARD

THE PIT OF FI

MALVEL'S MA

THE NIDREM CAVES

THE RIVER DOUR

KING
HUGO'S
PALACE

THE CITY

# STORY ONE

Greetings,

Welcome to my library, home to all manner of spell guides, potion books and records of Avantia's magical history. Only the most senior wizards and esteemed Avantian heroes are allowed entry to this hall of supreme knowledge.

Here on my shelves, you'll find the original volumes of the Book of the Beasts, out of the reach of those who would wish to steal them. It is my job to keep them safe, for thieving hands are always grabbing for knowledge that doesn't belong to them.

And those hands are reaching out for it now.

The Librarian

# CHAPTER ONE

# THE LIBRARY

Tom's sword clattered against the stone walls as he descended the narrow staircase. It was so dark he could barely make out Aduro just a few steps ahead.

"I can't believe there are still parts of this palace that are a mystery to us," said Elenna from behind him.

Aduro chuckled. "There are parts of the palace that even I don't know about," he told them.

"You still haven't told us where we're going," said Tom.

Aduro stopped on the stairs. The former wizard was breathing heavily and leaning on the wall.

"Are you all right?" asked Elenna.

"Just…getting my breath back," said Aduro. "I'm an old man now – no more magicking myself to places."

Tom's anger flared. The corrupt Judge of the Wizard Circle had stripped Aduro of his powers. Now Aduro's apprentice Daltec was the kingdom's young wizard.

"Almost there now," said Aduro, setting off again.

They reached a wooden door studded with iron bolts. Aduro drew a great rusty key from his robes and slotted it into the lock.

Tom held his breath as the door

slowly creaked open.

"Welcome to the library," said Aduro.

Tom heard Elenna gasp behind him. The room was huge, larger even than King Hugo's throne chamber. Oil lamps on brass stands threw a yellow glow over thousands of books bound in leather. Shelves stretched the length of the library into the gloom. Tom couldn't even see the far wall!

A shadow peeled itself from a desk and glided towards them.

In the lamplight, Tom made out a hunched, hooded figure. He felt a tickle of fear.

"Greetings, Librarian," said Aduro.

"These two are strangers," she said, her voice wet and rasping. "No strangers must enter the library."

"The library welcomes wizards and

heroes, does it not?" said Aduro. "Tom is Master of the Beasts, and Elenna is his brave companion."

The librarian sighed and shuffled back to her table, where an open book lay beside a water jug. "Very well," she muttered. "Keep the noise down."

Aduro bent his head close to Tom's. "The library's keepers are often selected from the non-magical children of wizards. They have knowledge of magical people and worlds, but no magical powers of their own. It makes them bitter."

"She doesn't look much like a child," Tom whispered.

"This librarian has served since before I was Avantia's Wizard," said Aduro. "She still treats me as a youngster!"

"So why are we here?" said Elenna.

Aduro smiled, and his eyes twinkled mischievously. "Because three pairs of eyes are better than one," he said. "We're looking for the eighth, nineteenth and thirty-third volumes of the *Chronicles of Avantia*. Daltec believes they hold a secret to assist with one of his potions."

"Won't they be shelved together?" asked Tom.

Aduro chuckled, and drew a glance from the librarian. "I'm afraid not," he said. "Wizards and other magical folk have never been very organised. We don't need to be, because we can summon books by magic." He raised his gnarled hands, twirled his fingers, then let them drop limply to his side again. "I can't any more, of course."

Tom frowned. "I don't understand. If the books are arranged randomly, what does the librarian actually do?"

Aduro's face was suddenly serious. "She's more of a guard," he muttered. "Come, let's find these books."

*Why would a library need a guard?* Tom

16

wondered, as he set off between the looming shelves.

He quickly saw that Aduro was right. *These books are a mess!* Atlases of distant kingdoms sat alongside books on mythical creatures. Spell books were filed with pamphlets on rare plants. One section was entirely made up of piled scrolls, marked in an ancient script Tom thought might be Kayonian. There were books on forbidden magic, on beginners' magic, and on magic that could only be practised at certain times of the year. He ran his fingers along the dusty spines, looking for the *Chronicles*.

*This could take forever*, he thought.

*Oof!* Something landed on his foot.

Elenna stood before him, a shocked expression on her face.

"I found the thirty-third *Chronicle*," she said. "It's heavy!"

"I know!" said Tom.

Elenna laughed and stooped to retrieve the book. Tom bent at the same time and their heads clashed. He rubbed his forehead dizzily, then took the book Elenna offered him.

"How can we be so clumsy after this many Quests?" Elenna said.

Tom's laughter caught in his throat when he saw something strange. Some loose pages were sticking out

from a book on the bottom shelf. Tom grasped them. There were four sheets in all, and each showed a drawing of a different Beast, with a scribe's notes beside them in faded writing.

"These pages are torn from the *Book of the Beasts*," said Tom. "But I've never seen these creatures before."

Elenna peered over his shoulder as he held the pages near an oil lamp. She read the names aloud: "Nera... Falkor... Gulkien..."

Tom held the last page near the lamp. The picture was faded but it still chilled his blood – a Beast taller than the ancient oaks of the Forest of Fear, with blue skin stretched taut across rippling muscle. The Beast's face looked like a mess of flesh and bone – Tom couldn't see any features at all.

"Anoret," Tom whispered.

# CHAPTER TWO

# AN ENEMY IN DISGUISE

They found Aduro five aisles over, his
nose in a scroll.

"Have you found the *Chronicles*?" he
asked.

"We found these," said Tom,
showing him the sheets of
parchment.

Even in the dim light, Tom saw
the colour drain from Aduro's skin.

He rolled up the scroll he had been looking at and placed it back on the shelf, then took the pages from Tom.

"What are these Beasts?" said Elenna. "We've never heard of them."

"No one is supposed to know about them," said Aduro in a low voice. "These pages aren't from the *Book of the Beasts* you've seen, but an older version. Nera, Falkor, Anoret and Gulkien belong to another time, since before Tanner, first Master of the Beasts."

"Tanner rode on Epos, didn't he?" asked Tom.

Aduro nodded. "The Flame Bird was known as Firepos then. Alongside Tanner fought three other heroes, whose names supposedly appear in the first four books of the Chronicles. Together the four heroes and four Beasts protected the kingdom."

"And what about that Beast?" said Elenna, pointing to Anoret.

"Little is known of Anoret," said Aduro. "Some say she was the very first Beast of Avantia, and mother to all others. Legend has it that she's buried somewhere under the Stonewin Volcano," He squinted at the page. "It says here that a warlord used her powers for evil." Aduro shrugged. "It's hard to know exactly what happened for certain. Stories change and—"

*Oof!*

A book came spinning from the darkness and smacked into the back of Aduro's head. The pages flew from his hands and Tom just managed to catch the wizard as he fell to the floor.

"He's out cold!" Tom said.

The scattered pages swirled up from the floor and drifted through the air past the shelves. Tom watched them sail off…

…right into the outstretched hands of the librarian.

"What have you done to our friend?" asked Elenna, kneeling beside Aduro.

The librarian gave a rasping chuckle as she slipped the pages inside her cloak. "No more than the old man deserved," she said.

Tom leaped up, drawing his sword. "You won't get away with this!" He strode towards her.

The librarian raised both arms and muttered some words under her breath. Tom ducked as a book shot from the shelf on his left and smacked into the wall opposite.

*Aduro was wrong! This librarian definitely has magical powers!*

More heavy books ripped themselves from the shelf, pelting into Tom's legs and body. Each blow made him cry out in pain.

The librarian gave a maniacal laugh. Pages torn from books fluttered through the air, blinding Tom, but Elenna appeared beside him with an arrow nocked to her bow. "Stop this!" she yelled.

The librarian sent a flurry of books

at Elenna, who ducked behind a
shelf. She peered out and fired an
arrow at their attacker. At the last
moment a thick book flew out and
caught the arrow-point. The shaft fell
harmlessly to the floor, its tip buried
in the leather cover.

As Elenna drew another arrow from her quiver, Tom raised his shield and ran at the librarian. Books slammed into the wood of his shield, sending painful shocks through his shoulder. But Tom gritted his teeth and careered headlong at the sorceress.

She shrieked as they collided, and fell across her desk. Tom landed beside her, then scrambled up and drew his sword.

"It's over!" he said. "Yield!"

Another cruel laugh came from beneath the hood. "It's not over," she said. "This is just the beginning!"

"Who *are* you?" Tom asked, keeping his sword-tip trained at her throat.

The librarian reached up slowly, and pulled down her hood. Long red hair tumbled loose, and two devious eyes glared at him, full of hate.

Tom almost dropped his sword in shock.

*How can it be…?*

"Kensa!"

## CHAPTER THREE

# DEADLY BOOKS

The sorceress was smiling. Tom hadn't seen her for a while, but he'd known she was lurking in Avantia somewhere.

"But...how did you... I don't..."

"Lost for words?" said Kensa. "I thought you'd be glad to see me again." She sat up, and Tom followed her every movement with his blade.

"What have you done with the real

librarian?" Elenna asked.

"Don't worry about her," Kensa
said. "I slipped a little something into
her milk at breakfast. She'll be asleep

for another few days, but she'll wake up. Probably."

"What do you want?" Tom asked.

"What does *anyone* want?" Kensa asked. "Power. And now I've got it."

"On your feet," said Tom.

Sighing, Kensa struggled upright and threw off her brown cloak. Beneath it she wore her black fur-lined robes, marked with stars and strange symbols picked out in golden thread. "I'm glad to get out of that smelly old thing," she said.

"Turn around," said Tom. "We're going to the dungeon, and it's even smellier there."

"I don't think so," said Kensa, grinning. She waved her hand like she was swatting a fly.

"Look out!" screamed Elenna.

Tom felt a shadow fall over him.

The shelves to his side were leaning over, toppling towards him. He dived aside as the wood and books smashed into the ground, throwing up a cloud of dust and spiders' webs.

*They would have crushed me!*

Kensa swished her hand again, and another shelf tumbled over. Tom rolled backwards out of the way. He dashed to Elenna's side, and hooked his arms under Aduro's shoulders.

"We need to get him to safety," Tom said.

Elenna took the wizard's feet. As more shelves crashed to the ground around them, Tom and Elenna carried Aduro to a recess. He moaned softly.

"Stay here with him!" Tom said.

"What are you going to do?" asked Elenna.

Tom drew his sword. "I'm going

to teach Kensa a lesson that's not covered in books."

He ran out, sliding beneath a toppling shelf. Books lay everywhere among piles of splintered wood, as Kensa directed the chaos. Tom stumbled through a fallen stack. "Stop this!" he bellowed. "Stand and fight fair!"

"Why fight fair when I can have fun?" Kensa said. She spread both palms and raised them upwards. Tom gasped as four books rose from the mess on the floor, their pages open and flapping like wings. The first swooped towards Tom, batting him in the chest and almost knocking him over. Then the second dived at his head. Tom managed to raise his elbow and deflect it. More books rose up like a flock of deadly birds.

Tom lifted his shield and tried to
batter through the assault, but the
books came at him, thudding into the
wood, driving him back like hammer
blows. He staggered backwards,

almost tripping, and peered over his shield's rim. Hundreds of books filled the air. *Too many*, he thought. *I need another plan.*

Tom sheathed his sword, turned and ran. Kensa cackled madly as she sent books slamming into his back and legs.

A book thumped into the side of Tom's head, knocking him dizzy. He just managed to stumble back to where Elenna cradled Aduro.

The old wizard's eyelids were fluttering, his face in a grimace as though he was suffering a bad dream. Three books shot past their heads, and circled in the upper reaches of the library.

*They're looking for me…*

Tom felt a tug at his side as Elenna reached for his sword and started to

rise. Tom grabbed her wrist. "No!"
he said. "These books hold precious
magic. We can't destroy them. We
have to get close to Kensa."

"But how?" said his friend.

Tom saw a fallen bookcase nearby.
He couldn't lift it alone, but maybe
both of them could.

"I've got an idea," he said.

Drawing his sword himself, he
threw it with a clang into the aisle
where Kensa would see it. "I yield!"
he cried out.

Elenna's eyes widened in alarm.

"Trust me!" Tom whispered. He
quickly told her his plan, and she
nodded grimly.

"Come out where I can see you!"
shouted Kensa. "You and the girl."

While the flying books flapped past,
Tom crept out from their hiding place

and gestured for Elenna to follow. He nodded at the bookcase. "Now!"

They each grabbed a side of the shelves and hoisted them in front as a shield.

"Fools!" said Kensa, thrusting out both arms.

Flying books hurtled towards them and crashed into the bookcase. Tom and Elenna rushed at the sorceress, whose face creased in panic. But a pile of scattered books stood in the way. As they reached it, Tom yelled "Drop the shelves!" and Elenna did as he asked. The bookcase fell over the pile of books like a ramp and Tom ran up it. Kensa was backing away. Tom unhooked his scabbard, lifted it two-handed over his head and leaped at the sorceress.

*If I can just knock her unconscious…*

He thought he'd won as he brought the heavy scabbard down, but at the last moment Kensa drew her silver Lightning Staff from her robes. Tom's makeshift weapon clashed against the metal of the staff and threw off a

great shower of sparks.

"I've been waiting for this," said Kensa, as she pushed him back. She fought fiercely, wielding her staff with power and accuracy. Tom managed to roll away as the staff crunched into a fallen shelf, reducing it to splinters.

*She's a better fighter than any of King Hugo's knights*, he thought.

"Here!" said Elenna.

Tom turned and saw his sword arcing towards him. He snatched it from the air by the hilt.

"Crafty!" sneered Kensa. "But it won't be enough."

Tom swung his sword at her shoulder, but the staff met it again with a ringing clang. As he pressed forward, another book flew through the air and thumped into his stomach. The wind rushed from his

lungs and Tom sank to one knee.
Kensa's gloating face loomed over
him and she raised her staff.

"Time to die, boy," she said.

"Not today!" shouted Elenna,
leaping over Tom and delivering
a flying kick to Kensa's side. The
sorceress lost her footing and tumbled
over with a wail.

Elenna aimed another kick,
bringing her heel down, but Kensa
dodged to one side. Tom found his
feet as Elenna continued her attack.
Her feet were blurs, each one driving
their enemy back a little more. Then
Kensa caught her foot and tossed
Elenna aside with a grunt. Tom saw
his friend fall heavily among the
fallen books. She climbed to her
knees, dazed.

Tom scrambled to Elenna's side.

"Are you all right?"

"Enough of this playing!" said Kensa. Tom glanced up and saw her holding one of the lanterns in her hand. The light played over her features, making them cast dancing shadows. "If you love books so much, I suppose you don't want to see this place burn to the ground."

"You wouldn't…" said Tom.

Kensa's grin widened, revealing a glint of white teeth. "Watch me!"

She threw the lantern against a wall. Glass exploded and flames fell on the stacks of fallen books, taking hold at once.

"Deal with that!" Kensa said. With a swirl of robes, she dashed through the open door and up the stairs.

# CHAPTER FOUR

# HUNTING THE HUNTER

Flames spread over the books, climbing higher.

"We can't let her escape!" said Elenna.

*But we can't let the library burn,* thought Tom.

He rushed to where Kensa had discarded the librarian's robes and snatched them up. He grabbed the pitcher of water from the librarian's desk and poured water over the cloak. More books were catching fire all the time, and the flames crackled as the pages burned. Tom threw the wet robe over the flames, batting them down. Elenna joined him, stamping her feet on any embers that remained. Soon the fires were out, and the air was filled with choking smoke. Tom tossed the scorched robes aside and saw that many of the books had been damaged. Their covers were half gone, their pages turned to ash.

"It could have been much worse," said a weak voice.

Aduro was standing behind them, leaning against a wall.

"Look after him," said Tom.

Before Elenna could reply he was on the stairs, taking them three at a time.

*Kensa must pay for this…*

Tom's legs were burning with exhaustion when he emerged into the dim light of a windowless room beside the stables. At the door, a young groom was nursing a cut to his head and pointed towards the courtyard. "She went that way," he muttered.

Tom ran into the courtyard and skidded to a halt.

High above the courtyard hovered Sanpao's pirate ship. Its blood-red sails were raised and the Beast's skull emblem fluttered on the canvas. Kensa dangled from a rope ladder hung from the bow, and Sanpao was hauling it towards the salt-stained hull. The Pirate King's oiled hair glistened in the sun, and the tattoos across his muscular arms bulged and shifted as he worked to heave Kensa

up, hand over hand.

*She's getting away!*

"Archers!" Tom roared. "Archers to the walls!"

Soldiers came running, spreading out along the edges of the courtyard and around the top of the battlements.

Kensa scrambled over the deck rail.

*It's going to be too late…*

"Take us about!" bellowed the Pirate King. "Full sail!"

The first arrows shot from the walls, thunking into the hull as the pirate ship turned slowly in the air with a creak of timbers. The sails snapped taut as the wind caught them.

Elenna appeared at Tom's side with Aduro leaning on one of her shoulders. She carried a lantern in the other hand. Her eyes took in the scene quickly. "Aim for the sails!" she shouted to the archers.

Arrows flew from the walls, but already some were falling short. One or two weakly shredded a sail, but Tom could see it wouldn't be enough to stop their enemies.

Elenna stood apart from Aduro, and

held an arrow point to the lantern's flame. She stretched her bowstring taut, and lined up the shaft. But her shot fell short, the arrow dropping and the flame dying when it hit the ground.

Tom punched his fist into his open palm. "Kensa escaped with the parchment... We've failed."

Aduro gazed into the sky, his eyes crinkled with concern. "We have lost this battle," he said, "but if I'm right about those pages, the war has only just begun. Come, Tom, we must summon the King."

A fire burned in the hearth of King Hugo's throne room. Standing before it, Tom stared into the flames, feeling his anger grow. *Just when the kingdom*

*seemed at peace, Evil has returned.*

And where was Aduro? He'd asked them to gather there while he went back to the library, but that had been hours ago.

"Will the librarian be all right?" asked the King.

Daltec, Aduro's apprentice, nodded. "Kensa's spell was a simple one. I've woken the librarian and she can't remember anything. It's better that way."

"She's going to get a nasty surprise when she goes back to work," said Elenna.

The door opened and Aduro paced in, clutching a battered book. *At last*, thought Tom.

The old wizard seemed to have fully recovered from his knock on the head, and his eyes were alive.

"What's this all about?" asked the King.

Aduro held the book so all of them could see. It looked like it was falling apart. "The *Journals of Tanner*," he said.

"The First Master of the Beasts!" said Daltec.

"Ancient legends?" said King Hugo.

Aduro laid the book on a table and faced the King. "All legends hold elements of truth. I was looking for information about Anoret, the First Beast. Sadly, much of the book is damaged, or the ink is faded. For centuries, Avantia's enemies have sought to bring Anoret back from her final resting place in the bottom of our volcano. In Tanner's day, she once submitted to an evil sorcerer called Derthsin. But no one knows what magic he used to control her."

Tom suddenly understood. "Kensa wants power over the First Beast!"

Aduro nodded. "The stolen parchment pages may well tell her how to get it."

"But why were they torn out?" asked Elenna.

Aduro patted Tanner's *Journal*. "That's what I've discovered. Tanner says he removed the pages and burned them, in order that no one should have power over Anoret."

"But he didn't burn them," said Tom. "They were in the library."

Aduro shrugged. "My guess is that he couldn't bring himself to destroy the pages after all, so he hid them where they wouldn't be found."

"Until now," said Daltec.

Tom felt his heart sink. "And we led Kensa right to them," he said.

Aduro placed a wrinkled hand on Tom's shoulder. "Evil cannot be stopped," he said. "All we can do is face it when it comes."

"But we don't even know where Kensa is!" said Elenna.

"We should go to my chamber," said Daltec. "The crystal ball might…"

A sudden pain shot through Tom's head, making his knees weak. A red glow, brighter than ever, shone from the ruby in his jewelled belt. A voice

drummed into his mind. Epos the
Flame Bird's voice.

*Evil approaches... Come quickly...*

"Epos is in trouble," Tom said. "We
have to get to Stonewin Volcano. That
must be where Kensa is heading!"

"And it's where Anoret is buried,"
said Elenna.

"Then that is where your Quest
lies," said Aduro. "Let us hope Kensa
doesn't have the magic to awake this
Beast of old."

"And if she does?" said King Hugo.

Aduro shook his head. "Then
your kingdom is in grave peril, Your
Highness."

Tom gripped the ruby and closed his
eyes, sending a message back to the
Flame Bird. *Have courage, old friend.*
*We're coming to your aid.*

# CHAPTER FIVE

# MONSTERS OF OLD

The air shuddered, and Tom's vision swam back into focus as Daltec's transportation spell faded. There were trees all around them, and a coating of pine needles on the ground. Tom was glad to see Elenna at his side, along with Storm and Silver. The horse whickered happily and the wolf pressed his muzzle into Elenna's hand. Daltec was the last to appear, a few

paces above the ground. He landed
with a thump.

"Ouch… Where are we?" said the
young wizard.

Tom stared about them into the trees
and realised where they *weren't*.

"This isn't Stonewin," he said, feeling
a flash of frustration.

Daltec blushed. "I'm still getting the

hang of my spells. It's hard when there are people and animals to move."

Tom took a few paces to the edge of the trees, and saw it was more of a small copse than an actual forest. Below them, a clutch of houses crowded by a river's side. Smoke rose from the chimneys and farm animals ran around behind fences.

"That's Rokwin, isn't it?" asked Elenna. "I remember the bridge."

"You're right," said Tom. "That means we're just south of the volcano." He turned and peered past the trees. Sure enough, Stonewin loomed over the landscape.

"Let's hope Kensa hasn't reached the volcano yet," he said. "We must be quick." He seized Storm's reins and climbed onto the horse's back. Elenna mounted behind him.

"I'll meet you there," said Daltec. "My magic works better if I'm alone."

The young wizard's lips moved in a spell, and he vanished, leaving only a trail of purple smoke.

"The quickest route goes through Rokwin and the other villages," Tom said. "But I don't want to raise any alarm. We'll go cross-country."

He kicked Storm into a gallop and they set off across the fields, leaping walls and fences and small streams. Silver streaked along beside them, tongue lolling as he ran. Tom could feel the ruby pulsing at his waist.

*Danger is coming… She is stirring.*

"Anoret…" Tom muttered beneath his breath. He'd never felt Epos so afraid. *But why is she afraid of Anoret? If Aduro was right, Anoret's the mother of all Beasts. She's not evil…*

The volcano reared taller all the time. Soon they were cantering through areas of hardened black stone where Stonewin had once spilled its lava. Tom dared not push Storm any faster in case he turned an ankle or cast a shoe.

As they rounded a small hillock, Sanpao's ship appeared ahead of them. The keel was dipping slightly as it descended towards Stonewin's crater.

*I hope we're not too late...*

They reached a steep incline, weather-worn, and Tom urged Storm up. The stallion's hooves skittered on the narrow path and Tom's knuckles grew white on the reins.

Finally, they reached a wider track. They heard squawks and shrieks mingled with pirate cries and Sanpao's bellowed orders.

"Come on," Tom said, pressing his knees into Storm's sides. "We need to get there, quick!"

As they crossed a ridge, a cold wind gusted around them and Tom glimpsed the shattered crater of the volcano. Sanpao's ship criss-crossed the sky in a deadly game of cat and mouse with Epos the Flame Bird. Pirates armed with crossbows and catapults sent

missiles hurtling at the Good Beast as she circled and swooped.

Sanpao's ship dropped suddenly out of reach. More crossbow bolts flew towards Epos, but her flames burned them to ashes.

Anger erupted through Tom.

"They won't do this to Epos," he said forcefully. "Whilst there's blood in my veins, she won't suffer!"

# CHAPTER SIX

# THE BEAST OF STONEWIN

A group of pirates landed on the crater's edge, and Kensa stood amongst them, her cloak whipped by the fierce wind and her staff planted on the ground.

*Her Lightning Staff,* Tom thought. *If it wasn't for lightning magic, she wouldn't even be here in Avantia and Aduro would still have his powers.*

Tom ran up the slope towards the sorceress with Elenna and Daltec at his side. The pirate band gathered to bar their path. They clutched whips and deadly throwing stars. Tom lifted his shield.

"Let me past and you won't be harmed," he said.

"Let him past and I'll have you all keelhauled until your backs are bloody!" roared Sanpao.

On the deck of his ship, several pirates were carrying something between them. Tom couldn't make out what it was.

"Take us up!" roared Sanpao.

The ship suddenly rose in the air, sailing above the Flame Bird. Only then did Tom see what they held.

*A net…*

Tom touched the ruby to send the

Good Beast a message. *Epos – fly!*

The Flame Bird flapped her wings hard, but at the same time the pirates hurled the net over the side. It opened like a sail and fell over Epos's body. Her wings curled and writhed, but the Flame Bird dropped like a stone back into Stonewin's crater. Her shrieks

echoed through the air.

"No!" shouted Tom.

"Rid of that pest at last!" shouted Sanpao. He leaned over the rail. "How much longer do we have to wait?"

"It'll take longer if you keep pestering me, you great brute!" Kensa bellowed back.

"She's trying to reawaken Anoret!" Elenna said, realising Kensa's plan.

Tom rushed at the centre of the band, cutting wildly with his sword to drive his enemies back. As the pirates lashed and stabbed at him, he dodged and deflected the blows. Through the fight, he saw Kensa pointing her staff at the side of the volcano, moving it in strange patterns.

One pirate was hurling his throwing stars with both hands. A star sank its jagged teeth into Tom's shield, and he saw another whistle past Daltec's face. Tom shoved the stinking pirate aside, sending him rolling down the slope. "Give up!" he yelled, pointing his sword at Kensa.

"Can you hear something?" Kensa called to Sanpao. "It sounds like a fly, buzzing in my ear." She continued twirling her staff.

"You don't know what you're meddling with," said Daltec. "Anoret is too much for you to control."

"You know, I think I hear another fly!" shouted Sanpao. "Why don't we swat them, my sweet?"

Kensa laughed. A red glow was forming on the side of the volcano where she was pointing her staff.

*Almost like the rock is melting…*

"What now?" asked Elenna.

Tom looked on desperately.

"Elenna! Daltec! Give me cover."

"Kill that little wretch!" screamed Kensa. "I'm almost there!"

The pirates charged, bellowing battle cries.

Bolts of blue light struck two pirates in the chest, knocking them off their feet. *Good work, Daltec*, Tom thought. Elenna wielded her bow like a staff, felling another pirate with a blow to the temple. Tom tripped one with his sword and barged another aside with his shield. Suddenly he was through. He turned back and saw Elenna and Daltec engaged in a fierce fight, but there wasn't time to stop and help. He began clambering towards the ledge where Kensa was working her sorcery.

*While there's blood in my veins, I have to stop her...*

The face of the volcano was white hot now, and the layers of rock were sliding over one another. Orange light bathed Kensa's face, and her smile was twisted and cruel. Tom stumbled behind her and raised his sword…

Kensa swung her staff around, and a bolt of magic slammed into Tom's

chest. It lifted him from the ground
and dumped him on his backside ten
paces away. A cry escaped his lips
and for a short while there was only
dizziness and pain.

He stood up and his legs were
shaking.

*No...not my legs...*

It was the *ground* shaking.

A low rumble seemed to spread
across the mountainside, as tears
appeared in the volcano. Rocks
sprayed from the hole.

Tom felt a voice speaking to him
through his ruby, but it wasn't Epos.
Or any of the other Good Beasts. This
voice was laced with ancient power
and made his very bones tremble.

*Behold! Anoret is arisen!*

Cracks snaked from the hole across
the rocky ground. Kensa staggered,

though she managed to keep her staff levelled at the volcano. Tom tried to keep his balance too, but when the ground collapsed to his left, he lost his footing. He tumbled down the slope. The world was a blur as he rolled over and over. Finally he managed to jam his blade into a fissure in the rock and stop his fall.

He found himself back near Elenna, Daltec and the pirates. Everyone was staring up the slope with their mouths hanging open.

Black and yellow smoke swirled from the open rockface. A giant claw emerged, thick and discoloured and as long as Tom was tall. It was followed by a stubby foreleg, coated in green scales that looked as thick as armour. Tom's breath caught in his throat as more claws followed.

They tore at the ground as the Beast
heaved herself out into the open.

Anoret was like nothing Tom had ever seen. She reminded him of a reptile or a dragon. She was crawling, her jointed hind legs thick as tree trunks but dragging over the ground. Each one ended in three vicious claws, caked with dirt. Rows of red spikes bristled along her spine. Her scaly blue face was like a lizard's, snub-nosed with slashes for nostrils and fiery blood-red eyes. And her jaws were like a shark's, filled with razor-sharp dagger teeth.

# CHAPTER SEVEN

# BORN OF FIRE

Anoret tried to stand, pushing herself up on her front legs, but crashed to earth again, making the mountain shake. The pirates were clutching each other in fear.

"What in all the High Seas is that?" one cried.

*No wonder she's weak*, thought Tom. *She's been asleep for four hundred years!*

The final part of the Beast to slide

from her lair was her tail, thick and powerful and covered in more leathery green scales. She lifted it and thumped it down hard, smashing the rock at her feet. Her massive head swayed from side to side, surveying the chaos. As she turned, Tom saw something strange. Around the edges of her eyes and jaw was a line of ragged, raised scar tissue. It looked like an old wound, badly healed, where the skin had been torn open.

Tom shuddered. *What happened to you?* he wondered.

Sanpao's pirates were backing away, and on board his ship, Tom spotted the Pirate King leaning over the rail, as awestruck as everybody else.

Kensa was walking right up to the Beast.

Anoret lifted her head, and her

jaws parted. White spittle stretched between them, and a narrow pink tongue flickered out.

*What's Kensa doing?* thought Tom. *She's going to get herself killed!*

Anoret roared, blasting Kensa with a breath that made the sorceress stagger back.

But Kensa kept coming, and lifted her staff before her.

"Surely she's not going to fight the Beast?" whispered Elenna.

"No," said Daltec. "If Aduro was right, she's got other plans."

A bolt of silver light crackled from Kensa's staff, striking Anoret's face. Sparkling light spread over the Beast's features. Anoret growled and shook her head wildly from side to side, as if she was trying to pull herself free. Kensa gripped her

staff two-handed and the silver light
shone brighter still.

"Give yourself to me!" Kensa

screeched as she directed the light.

Anoret's growls became a low moan, as if she was being ripped apart from the inside. One foreleg thumped into the ground, and then her hind leg bent as well. Slowly, with the magic still latched onto her face and Kensa shaking from head to toe, the Beast began to stand. She was three times as tall as Nanook and her scales glittered like polished gemstones.

"Something's happening in there," one of the pirates muttered.

Tom saw it too. In the heart of the silver glow, Anoret's face was changing, stretching outwards towards Kensa's staff. With a wet and hideous sound, the skin tore loose. Anoret's screams stabbed into Tom's ears. All around him, pirates

81

clutched their heads and fell to their knees. When Tom managed to look up, a scaly mask was floating down through the air towards Kensa. Its empty eyeholes gaped above nostril slits and sagging lips.

What it left behind turned Tom's stomach.

Where Anoret's face had been he now saw raw flesh, jutting bones and bare muscle. Anoret's clawed forelegs rose to her disfigured features as if trying to conceal them.

*As if she's ashamed.*

Tom felt a stab of pity for this terrifying Beast, but it was quickly drowned by the voice of Epos, coming from deep in Stonewin's crater.

*Do not let the woman wear Anoret's face… The Mask of Death must not fall into the wrong hands.*

Tom bounded up the slope. The
Mask was drifting gently towards
Kensa and she'd put aside her staff,
raising her hands to claim it. Tom
ran into her, pushing her away and
making her stumble and trip over the
rocks.

"No! It's mine!" she screeched.

The Mask floated into Tom's hands.

As soon as his fingers touched it, the flesh stiffened and shrank to the size of his own head. He felt the power flowing through it, and he knew then that if he put it on he would never take it off again…

*Whack!*

Pain scorched across Tom's shoulders and he dropped the Mask at his feet. He staggered forwards, reaching for his sword, and when he turned, Sanpao stood there, one hand clutching a rope and another holding his vicious whip with several leather thongs.

"This belongs to us!" he said, picking up the Mask.

"It belongs to no one but the Beast," Tom snapped back.

For a moment, Sanpao seemed to pause, staring into the eye sockets of the Mask in his hands.

"Give it to me!" yelled Kensa, striding towards the Pirate King.

Sanpao trailed his filthy fingers lovingly across the Mask. "It's beautiful…" he muttered.

Kensa snatched it from him and in one swift movement, she slipped the Mask over her face. Immediately, the scales seemed to clench over her cheeks and harden as they moulded to her features. Her back arched and her hair seemed to glow even more brightly than before. She hissed as she

drew a breath and stretched out her arms.

"Oh, oh, it's wonderful!" she said.

Anoret suddenly became still. Tom knew she was under Kensa's control now.

"Let's get out of here," said Sanpao. He gave a whistle and the men on board his ship hoisted him skywards. The other pirates seized dangling ropes of their own and scrambled aboard.

Kensa turned to face Tom, her eyes blazing behind the Mask. "It's all over," she said softly. "Anoret is mine!"

"It's never over," said Tom. "Whatever you're planning, I'll stop you."

Kensa laughed, then ran to a ledge and leapt off, somersaulting through the air and landing on deck.

"To Rion!" she cried.

Wind caught the sails, and the pirate ship began to drift away. Below them, on the ground, Anoret moved too, her huge body thundering across the slopes of Stonewin, directly beneath her new mistress.

"Rion?" said Elenna. "Why there?"

"Rion is home to all the young Beasts," said Tom. "The future protectors of the kingdoms. Kensa and Sanpao must be planning to turn them Evil. We have to follow and stop them."

"Aduro mentioned that there's a new Beast Keeper," Elenna said. "Wilfred, I think."

Silver suddenly growled, and bared his teeth.

"Oh no," said Daltec, pointing to the ridge behind them.

Tom saw them too. Two creatures

side by side on the crest of the slope ahead. They were twice the size of Silver, with matted grey fur, hunched backs, and yellow tusks growing from their lower jaws.

"Varkules!" whispered Elenna.

One of the Varkules reached out its long claws and tore at the rock with them. Slaver drooled from its teeth. Tom's throat became dry. They'd faced these fearsome creatures before. They were monsters from a forgotten age – long extinct, but brought back to terrifying life by the darkest, most evil of spells.

*Anoret's return must have summoned them too.*

Tom looked around. "There are only two," he said, his hand slipping to his sword hilt. "It won't be easy, but we can defeat them."

The words had barely left his
mouth when more shapes appeared
on the ridge. More of the hunched
attackers. Tom counted eight…no,
thirteen. Then he stopped counting.
It was a huge pack, and every
glowing eye was turned hungrily on

Tom and his companions.

"I'm not sure my magic will be enough," said Daltec.

"Or my arrows," said Elenna.

Tom clenched his fist over his ruby, feeling Epos's strength, the power of Stonewin. The Flame Bird soared above the volcano, her feathers roaring with flame. Strands of netting, charred and broken, hung from her feathers.

As she swooped towards the Varkules, they scattered beneath her blazing wings.

The Good Beast soared towards Tom and his friends.

*Can you take us to Rion, Epos?* Tom sent the thought out to the Good Beast.

The Flame Bird alighted beside them, her eyes shining. She dipped

her head in agreement. The battle
wasn't lost yet.

"To Rion!" Tom cried.

# STORY TWO

*You're as foolish as Tom!*

*You had no idea that I was in disguise. You cannot see evil when it lurks right before you. Your stupidity will be your downfall. It will also be the downfall of my wretched enemies, Tom and Elenna.*

*My minions and I fly to Rion, where young Beasts are raised to become Great Protectors. But we will change that. We will snare for ourselves more Beasts and train them to be our vicious servants.*

*If we can corrupt Anoret, we can surely bend any Beast-brat to our will. Our Beast army will be unstoppable! All the kingdoms will soon beg for our mercy.*

*Kneel before your new ruler!*
*Kensa the Witch*

# CHAPTER ONE

# RION IN PERIL

Daltec's face was green as he clung to Epos's feathers.

"I don't understand why we couldn't use magic to travel to Rion," he said.

"After last time, we had to be sure where we'd end up," said Tom, allowing himself a tiny flicker of a smile. It vanished quickly when he thought about the task ahead. An ancient Beast was marching on this kingdom, guided by hands of Evil. None of the young Beasts would be able to stand up to such deadly enemies.

*I have to help them.*

They were soaring high over the northern reaches of Avantia and into Rion. With all three of them plus the animals, Epos's broad back was

crowded, but it didn't seem to slow the Flame Bird down.

*She knows how important this Quest is,* thought Tom.

Cold wind whistled past, but Epos's feathers kept them warm. Storm lay on his side, and Silver curled between his legs. Tom kept a look out for either Sanpao's ship in the sky or Anoret on the ground below. *We might be too late…*

"What if Kensa was bluffing?" said Elenna. "She might have shouted 'Rion' to send us this way, when actually she's gone to Gwildor!"

Tom shook his head. "I doubt Anoret could swim that far," he said. "Besides, I have this." He tapped the ruby at his belt. "I can feel Anoret's anger. She came this way, I'm sure."

Epos suddenly dipped her wings

and started to descend.

*This is as far as I can go*, she told Tom through the ruby.

The Flame Bird landed just beyond the Nidrem caves, alighting on the banks of the fast-flowing River Dour.

"We haven't caught them yet," said Elenna, as she clambered off with Silver. "Why are we stopping here?"

"Epos is tired," Tom said.

"I don't mind getting off early," said Daltec, clutching his stomach. "I think I'm going to be sick."

Tom stroked the Flame Bird's neck as Storm leaped onto the grassy riverbank. "Thank you for bringing us this far," he said.

Epos sprang into the sky and flapped away. Soon she was just a speck climbing through the clouds.

Tom quickly mounted Storm. "I'll

ride from here to get word to Wilfred the Beast Keeper of what's coming. Daltec, use your magic to head there with Elenna and the animals. I'll be quicker, moving alone, and I'll be able to sense Anoret's feelings better if I don't have distractions."

He set off at a gallop, riding over fields and through glades, deep into Rion. It was a beautiful kingdom, almost always at peace – the perfect place to train young Beasts away from danger.

The light of day was beginning to fade. As he tore across open ground, Tom spotted a black speck in the sky ahead.

"Sanpao..." he muttered, driving Storm on faster. He imagined Anoret creeping across the kingdom below the ship. The Beast wasn't Evil by nature. *But as long as Kensa controls Anoret, I must consider her my enemy.*

He lost track of the ship in the gathering gloom of dusk, but he could still sense that Anoret was getting closer all the time – and she was burning with hatred and confused rage.

Then, as Tom came to the brow of a hill, he saw her. The Beast was thundering towards a small village about the same size as Rokwin. Sanpao's ship was hovering above, and lanterns on deck picked out the faces of Sanpao, Kensa and the pirate crew.

*Kensa's going to make Anoret destroy the village!* Tom realised.

He spurred Storm down the slope towards the Beast. He wasn't yet sure what he'd do when they met, but he couldn't stand by and watch innocent

people be killed. Anoret crushed
the first of the fences she reached,
swishing her club-like tail back and
forth. Chickens darted in panic from
the remains of their coop, and pigs
grunted as they fled beneath the
Beast's legs. People emerged from
their homes, screaming and shouting

in terror. Above it all, Tom could hear Kensa's mad cackle.

Anoret's tail lashed a watermill, reducing it to smashed timbers. She stamped carts and took the roof off a house with a single swipe of her claws. As Tom galloped in her wake, dust filled his eyes. He saw villagers, young and old, scattering from the remains of the buildings.

Tom drew his sword and charged beneath the Beast's legs. He swung his blade with all his might at the Beast's ankle, but it bounced harmlessly off the tough green scales. Anoret must have felt the blow though, because she roared and tried to swipe him off Storm's saddle with a scythe-like claw. Tom yanked Storm's reins sideways and the claw whooshed just past his head.

*I have to get her away from the village,
or these people are doomed.*

Storm galloped past the collapsed
mill. "Follow us, if you dare!" Tom
cried. Through the ruby, he felt
Anoret's anger swell, and the Beast
gave chase.

*It's working, but how long can I keep
running?*

Anoret's feet shook the ground as

she leaped in Tom's wake. Peering over his shoulder, Tom saw that the Beast was gaining, eyes narrowed to slits, and claws raking the air.

*Come back, you fool!* called a voice. *The boy's trying to trick you. You're mine, remember…*

It took Tom a moment to understand what he was hearing.

*Kensa! The ruby must be picking up her voice, because she's wearing the Mask!*

Anoret came to a sudden halt.

"Hey!" said Tom. "Come and get me!"

But the Beast stalked back towards the village.

*That's right*, said Kensa, smiling in triumph. *There's killing to be done here.*

Anoret stamped across the river and stabbed her claws into the ground beneath another house. With a roar, she ripped the whole building from the ground, and let it dangle from her fist before hurling it into the water. Tom hoped there was no one inside.

A shadow fell over Tom and his hand went to his sword hilt again. What new threat was this? He looked up and a cry of terror escaped his lips. Two dragons, each almost the size of Ferno, bore down on him, wings spread and smoke trailing from between their jagged teeth.

*This is the end*, he thought.

# CHAPTER TWO

# OLD FRIENDS

The dragons tipped back their wings, reached out with their claws, and landed either side of Tom.

*Master…* he heard. *Are we too late?*

Tom almost dropped his sword in shock as his eyes took in the familiar snouts and crests. One dragon was red, and the other was green. Could it be…?

"Vedra?" he said. "Krimon?"

*Hello again*, they said in unison.

Tom marvelled at their size. When he'd last seen the twin dragons they'd been babies, barely bigger than Storm. Now they were fearsome Beasts to be reckoned with.

"I need your help," Tom said, pointing towards the threatened village. "We must face Anoret."

*Leave it to us*, Krimon replied.

With a rush of air, both dragons took off and swept across the fields towards the village. Tom galloped after them.

Storm couldn't keep up with the dragons, who arrived first above the shattered houses of the settlement. Anoret was smashing her claws into the ground. Vedra blasted a spurt of fire towards the Beast, who shielded her face with her stubby arms.

Krimon sent another jet of flame, and Anoret staggered backwards, almost trampling a dog as it scampered out of one of the houses.

Tom heard a voice inside his own head, sweet and hissing. *Join me…*

it said. *Join the Mother of Beasts and be stronger than ever before…*

Vedra and Krimon paused in their attack, hovering uncertainly.

"Don't listen to her!" Tom called. "She's trying to turn you to Evil."

The twin dragons attacked again with fiery snorts. Anoret tried to swipe at them but she might as well have been swatting at flies. They veered in the air, and more spurts of

flame sent Anoret stumbling from the village, her scales scorched.

"Stay and fight!" Sanpao roared. "Lure the young Beasts over!"

But Anoret wasn't listening. Relief flooded Tom's heart as he watched the Beast break into a run across the fields, followed by the pirate vessel.

Vedra and Krimon gave chase a little way, then wheeled around and flew back to Tom.

"They'll be back," he said. "And next time Anoret won't be repelled so easily."

*We will be ready*, said Vedra.

Tom flushed with pride. He never would have dreamed the twin babies could become so courageous and powerful, and he was glad they'd managed to resist Anoret's temptations. It gave him an idea.

A risky one, but what other choice did he have?

*Wilfred has other Beasts in his care too. If I can train them as well, we'll be a force to be reckoned with.*

"Take me to the Beast Keeper," he said to the dragons. "It's time to defend Rion!"

The twin dragons escorted him away from the village and across a wide valley. Tom rode Storm hard to keep up. The stallion seemed to have found new strength since Anoret's retreat.

Vedra and Krimon descended towards the edge of a forest, where Tom saw a slender young man with wild red hair. *The Beast Keeper*, he thought. Wilfred was sitting on what looked like a muscular young bull.

At first Tom wondered if the creature was even a Beast, but as it turned towards the noise of Storm's hooves, he saw its stubby horns were encased in blue flames.

Wilfred was kicking the Bull Beast's flanks with his heels, obviously trying

to get it to move.

"Greetings!" Tom called, as he slowed Storm to a trot. The Beast snorted and bucked, throwing Wilfred from its back. The Beast Keeper landed with a grunt on the grass as the Beast charged off.

*Stop, Raffkor!* Vedra commanded.

The young Beast skidded to a halt.

*Vedra's turned into quite a leader,* thought Tom.

As Vedra and Krimon swooped away towards their mountain caves, Tom dismounted from Storm and offered a hand to Wilfred. Raffkor came trotting back, his blue horns glowing.

"I'm Tom," he said, tugging the red-haired man to his feet. "Avantia's Master of—"

"I know who you are," said Wilfred,

eyes goggling. "The honour is mine. But no one told me you were coming."

Tom patted Storm's neck. "We came in a rush," he said. "Pursuing Evil."

Wilfred's wide-eyed stare faded. "A Beast?"

Tom nodded. As quickly as he could, he explained the threat from Anoret that faced Rion and the young Beasts. He told Wilfred of Kensa and Sanpao too, and the ship that flew rather than sailing.

"I've heard of Anoret," Wilfred said when Tom had finished, "but I thought she was just a myth."

"I wish she were," said Tom. "I'm afraid she's real, and it won't be long until she wants to fight again. She's not Evil herself, but she's under the power of whoever wears her Mask –

and, right now, that's Kensa. I think the witch will try to corrupt the young Beasts too."

Raffkor stamped his hooves and tossed his massive head, and the flames of his horns flared brighter. Tom felt their heat baking his face.

"What's got into him?" he asked.

Wilfred moved closer to the Bull Beast, and laid his hand on Raffkor's neck. "I don't..."

In a puff of purple smoke, Daltec, Elenna and Silver appeared twenty paces down the slope. When Daltec saw Tom, he punched the air. "I'm getting better at this!"

"Third time lucky," muttered Elenna, rolling her eyes. "Tom, you wouldn't believe where we've—"

Her words turned to a scream, because suddenly Raffkor was

stamping towards them, churning up the ground with his hooves.

*No!* thought Tom desperately. *He's going to gore them!*

# CHAPTER THREE

# RAISING A BEAST ARMY

Wilfred tried to grab a horn, but Raffkor tossed him aside angrily and continued his charge. Tom didn't have time to check on the Beast Keeper.

*Stop!* he called to the young Beast through Torgor's ruby.

Raffkor came to a stop, hooves digging into the earth. He spun around, and his eyes flashed with anger. *He's angry and confused*, Tom thought. *I suppose he doesn't see people very often.*

*We're not your enemies*, Tom said.

The Beast lowered his horns and charged at Tom.

Tom had no choice. He drew his sword, and stepped aside at the last

moment, delivering a hard blow to Raffkor's horns. The Beast careered sideways but a painful shock wave sizzled up Tom's arms. He couldn't keep a grip on his sword.

*What in all of Avantia was that?* he thought.

Raffkor threw up clods of earth as he twisted to face Tom again. The blue flames on his horns had dimmed, Tom noticed.

*He must have used up some of his energy zapping me*, he thought. *That's his Beastly power…*

But the Bull Beast still had plenty in reserve. Raffkor snorted, stamped and charged again.

"Raffkor, no!" yelled Wilfred.

Without his sword, Tom lowered his shield. Surely the blow would smash it to pieces, but he had no choice. He braced himself for impact. *This is going to hurt…*

When Raffkor was ten paces away, a net fell over him, its strands golden and glowing. The Bull Beast tripped over its tangled hooves, thumped onto the ground and slid to Tom's feet.

Tom looked up from behind his shield and saw the net trailing from a magical golden rope leading to Daltec's open palms.

"Thanks!" Tom gasped. "That was close."

"You might not be great at navigation," said Elenna, "but you can pull out a good spell when it really matters."

Daltec smiled, his face flushing, and closed his fists. The net vanished. Raffkor shook himself and found his

feet, flanks heaving, but he didn't
attack again.

"Taught you a lesson, didn't they?"
said Wilfred, stepping up to the Beast
and stroking its head. "Maybe next
time you'll listen to me." He turned
to Tom. "Sorry about that – it's early
in his training and he's still a little…
um…restless."

Tom grinned, glad to see that the Beast Keeper was unhurt after his fall. His eyes went to the horizon, back the way they'd come.

"We might need all your Beasts to show courage like Raffkor," he said. "Anoret will be here soon."

Wilfred paled. "The Beasts are too young to fight her," he said. "Too inexperienced."

"Perhaps at the moment," said Elenna. "But with a little training, and working as a team, we might be able to stand up to Kensa's Beast."

Wilfred face creased into a frown. "I'm not sure…"

"It's the only chance we have," said Tom. "Summon the Beasts, Wilfred. Let's see what our new army is made of."

Tom watched the three shapes approach through the sky. They'd been training with the young Beasts for a good stretch of time and none of them were flagging yet. *They're hard workers*, Tom thought. *Just what I need in a battle!* In the centre was Falra, the white-feathered Phoenix, with Elenna lying close against her back. On either side were Vedra and Krimon.

Falra was only two years old, Wilfred had told them, but already Elenna had taught her to hover and wheel around sharply. *She'll need both skills if she's to avoid Anoret's claws*, Tom thought.

Now her snow-white wings were flapping madly as she struggled to keep up with the twin dragons.

Small flames smouldered over her feathers.

"Good work!" Tom called up.

Across the valley Tom saw Wilfred scrambling nimbly from branch to branch among the trees. He was being chased by a spindly Monkey Beast called Tikron. The Beast reminded Tom of Claw, only half the size, with pale grey fuzzy fur rather than matted brown.

"Help!" called Daltec. Tom turned and saw the Wizard apprentice being dragged across the ground, trying to dig in his heels. A golden rope stretched from his hands and the other end was held in the jaws of a giant red snake.

"It looks like Vislak is winning the tug of war!" Tom shouted.

"It's not fair!" Daltec yelled back. "He's bigger than me!" He lost his grip on the rope and landed on his backside. "Ouch!"

Vislak reared up his head and hissed in triumph.

Tom nodded proudly. Wilfred had selected the most promising of his Beast-students to form the last defence of Rion. Tom heard the thunder of hooves, and suddenly remembered the Beast he was supposed to be schooling. Raffkor was hurtling towards him, horns glowing and steam blasting from his flaring nostrils. Tom was holding a scrap of red velvet to attract the Beast.

*And something tells me this isn't a game to Raffkor…*

When the Beast was five paces away, Tom leaped straight up in the air. The power of his golden boots carried him over the Beast's back and he landed in the grass on the other side. Raffkor tried to turn quickly but lost his balance and tumbled over in a cloud of dust.

*He's quick, but clumsy*, Tom thought. *If he can control his anger, he'll be a deadly foe.*

The Bull Beast's horns flared

brighter as he righted himself and ran at Tom once more. Tom leaped sideways this time, and Raffkor shot past. He bellowed in frustration.

*You need to be more clever*, Tom said with his mind. *Fighting is not just about brute strength.*

Raffkor's horns glowed almost white and two blue bolts shot from their tips. They scorched the velvet in Tom's hands, turning it to ash.

Elenna landed beside Tom on Falra. As the Phoenix folded her majestic wings, Elenna laughed. "If Raffkor can do that, maybe we have a chance, after all."

Raffkor was tearing at the grass with his teeth. *He seems very pleased with himself...* Tom noticed that the blue flames had almost died away. *He needs time to build up his power again.*

*That will make him vulnerable.*

Suddenly Vislak's head jerked up from his coils and Tikron the Monkey Beast gave a burst of high-pitched shrieks.

"What is it?" Elenna said.

Storm snorted, tossing his head.

Daltec pointed a shaking finger across the valley, where a familiar shape was coming over the horizon: Sanpao's ship, blood-red sails flying.

"We need more time!" said Wilfred.

Tom gripped his sword hilt. "Time just ran out," he said.

# CHAPTER FOUR

# THE BATTLE BEGINS

Anoret's faceless head appeared over the crest of the valley, all tendon, gore and bone. Tom heard Wilfred gasp.

"What happened to her?" asked the Beast Keeper.

"Kensa has stolen her face," said Tom. "We need to give it back."

The huge Beast made her way towards them, each giant footstep shaking the ground.

"Storm, Silver, stay back," Tom commanded. This was a fight for Beasts, and he didn't want their faithful animals being harmed.

Storm tossed his head, obviously reluctant to obey, but Tom pointed into the trees. "Go!" The stallion and wolf slunk off together.

Tom ordered the six Beasts to

line up across the valley. Vedra and
Krimon took positions in the centre,
with Tikron and Falra on one side and
Vislak and Raffkor on the other. The
Monkey Beast thumped the ground
with his fists, and the white Phoenix
shrieked a battle cry. Raffkor was
churning earth with his hooves, eager
to fight.

"Hold steady!" Tom ordered. "We have to stay together."

*If we don't, Anoret and the pirates will pick us off, one by one.*

He stood beside Daltec, Elenna and Wilfred. A wizard, a warrior and a Beast Keeper, plus six young, powerful creatures. On any other day, he'd trust they were a match for Sanpao's pirates and a single Evil Beast. But Anoret was no ordinary foe. She was the First Beast, the most powerful. And if she, or Kensa, managed to corrupt any of Tom's new army, the tide would turn in an instant.

Tom saw the sorceress at the ship's prow, her Lightning Staff in hand and her locks flying. At her side, leaning over the rail, Sanpao gripped a rope.

*You can do this*, Tom told his Beasts.

*You can protect your kingdom.*

Anoret was still a hundred paces away when Vislak the snake shot forward in a rush of red scales.

*No!* Tom thought.

"Come back!" Wilfred cried.

But the crimson snake was fired by the foolish bravery of youth. He slithered forward in a rapid blur, his forked tongue shooting

towards Anoret's ravaged face. For a heartbeat, Tom thought the attack might work, but Anoret ducked just as quickly and fastened her teeth over Vislak's sinuous body. With a jerk of her head, the First Beast tossed Vislak high into the air.

"Vedra! Krimon!" Tom cried.

The Twin Dragons took off towards Vislak's falling coils.

*Three Beasts out of action already*, thought Tom, as Anoret stamped in their direction.

"Kill them all!" Kensa yelled.

No sooner had Vedra clasped Vislak in her claws than a hail of arrows sailed from the deck of the pirate ship. Vedra and Krimon dodged it in the air, but another volley followed the first. *Sanpao's keeping them at bay*, Tom realised. *We can't sit back and wait now… Our only hope is to overpower the Beast with numbers.*

"Attack!" he yelled, pointing with his sword at Anoret. He led the charge, sprinting across the grass towards the looming Beast. Anoret's gruesome face seemed to stretch into a lipless smile and she twisted suddenly. The great club of her tail swished around. Tom leaped over it in a somersault, and landed on the lowest spike on her back. She roared and shook, and he had to wrap his arms around the spike to hang on. *At least her teeth and claws can't get me here.*

Tom's bones shook as he clambered higher and Anoret thumped the ground with her tail. His sword was useless, so he used his shield to deliver blow after blow to Anoret's back. *If I can just reach her head, I might be able to knock her unconscious.*

He reached the topmost spike, and raised the shield to box the Beast's ears, when he felt a rush of air at his back. He threw himself clear, and Anoret's tail slammed right into the back of her own head. Tom rolled away across the grass as the Beast lumbered dizzily.

*That was harder than any strike I could have managed.*

As Anoret stumbled, Tom saw Tikron leap through the air with Wilfred clutching his back. The Monkey Beast drummed on Anoret's belly with his fists. Elenna guided Falra behind the faceless Beast, clawing at her back with her talons. Raffkor had joined the fray too, butting into Anoret's head, delivering shocks from his deadly horns.

Lights flashed in the sky. The pirate
ship rocked as purple bolts shot from
Daltec's hands, singeing the hull and
scorching holes through the sails. But
Kensa leaped onto the prow, staff
in hand. She fired a silver stream of
light at Daltec, scorching the grass

by his feet black. Daltec dived aside and came up in a crouch. He fired his magical bolts again. One smashed into the deck rail and Kensa fell back with a cry of alarm.

"Good shot!" cried Tom.

The arrows had stopped shooting from the deck as Krimon swooped low, releasing a jet of fire which set the mast aflame. Nearby, Vedra was laying Vislak down on the grass. Tikron had both arms wrapped around Anoret's neck, and Raffkor threw himself at his enemy's legs. Anoret bellowed and staggered under the attacks of the brave young Beasts.

*We're winning*, Tom thought. *We just have to force our advantage…*

Then his heart sank as a familiar chorus of snarls and grunts reached his ears. A row of Varkules filled the horizon, drool spilling from their tusks and yellow eyes flashing.

As Anoret roared, the Varkules charged down into the clearing like a great deadly wave.

## CHAPTER FIVE

# THE TIDE TURNS

Tom watched helplessly as the savage Varkules bounded towards them.

*The clearing seemed like such a good place to train the Beasts, but it's impossible to defend.*

Through Torgor's ruby, he sensed the confusion of the young Beasts. They didn't know where to take the fight, with so many opponents.

"Fall back!" Tom commanded.

"Vedra, Krimon, use your flames!"

The Twin Dragons swooped towards the sea of fur and tusks, snorting jets of fire. The Varkules' growls became yelps of fear as a group scattered before the flames. But just as many of the creatures kept coming.

Tom leaped at the line, slashing at

some with his sword and battering others with his shield. *If we fail now, Rion and Avantia are finished!* He heard a whistle in the air as an arrow sailed into the ravening pack. Another shaft followed, as Elenna picked off their enemies.

The others recoiled, snapping their teeth, but with their tails between their legs.

"That's it!" Tom called. "We're driving them back."

He smacked one of the ugly creatures on the muzzle and sent it scurrying away.

*We might just win this…*

*BOOM!*

The ground to Tom's left exploded in a shower of earth and tufts of grass. Even the Varkules ran away in fear. When the smoke cleared Tom saw a crater as deep as he was tall.

"Look out!" yelled Daltec.
"Cannon!"

Tom glanced up and saw Sanpao
lighting another fuse, and swinging
the barrel of the cannon to bear on
him. The pirate ship was burning in
places and its sails were shredded,
but the Pirate King wasn't finished
yet. More pirates were levelling the

ship's other cannons.

*BOOM!*

Tom dived to the ground as another iron ball ripped into the earth.

*BOOM! BOOM! BOOM!*

Through the raining debris, Tom saw Elenna running one way, and Wilfred another. Raffkor tripped and fell into a crater headfirst, and Falra's feathers were covered in soot. Vislak was hissing madly, slithering across the ground, and Tikron was howling at the sky.

*They've forgotten about Anoret!* Tom thought, getting up. *This isn't good…*

As Raffkor struggled from the crater, Kensa's Beast brought her tail around in a vicious swipe. The Bull Beast must have weighed as much as ten horses, but the tail knocked him upside down like a skittle. Anoret

lifted it again, ready to crush the life
from the brave bull.

"Vislak!" Tom shouted, as the Snake
Beast slithered across the clearing.
"The tail!"

The Snake Beast arched his neck
and darted with a sudden strike,
fastening his fangs over Anoret's
massive tail. At the same time, Tikron

swiped at Anoret's legs. Like a slowly toppling tree, the First Beast fell. When she hit the ground, it felt like an earthquake and Tom almost lost his balance.

Raffkor scrambled up and charged. He drove his glowing horns into the remains of Anoret's face. Blue light burst forth, and scraps of rotting flesh flew off the wound. Anoret roared and squirmed on the ground.

"That's it!" Tom said. "While there's blood in your veins, fight!"

He saw a flash of grey fur to his side and raised his shield just as a Varkule hurled itself at him. Its tusks tore gouges in the wood, and its teeth fastened over the rim. Tom tugged desperately to free his shield from the terrible jaws, almost retching as the creature's foul breath hit him.

Finally he delivered a fierce kick to its underbelly and the Varkule let go.

"Take us down!" yelled Kensa.

As the Varkules gathered around Tom and Elenna, the mighty pirate ship began to dip its prow and descend.

"We can't let them land!" yelled Elenna. "If Kensa gets close to the other Beasts with her Mask, she could turn all of them to Evil."

Tom swiped at a Varkule with the flat of his blade and it scampered away with a whimper. But the others pressed forward, snarling. Tom sensed yet more at his back and a quick glance confirmed it. *We're being surrounded.*

Worse still, Anoret had Falra in her jaws. She tossed the Phoenix aside like a plaything and pulled herself onto all fours. She leaned back and tore Vislak's fangs from her tail in a shower of blood. Tikron tried to leap at the First Beast's face, but Anoret caught him in midair with a blow from the back of her hand that sent him flying through the air.

The Varkules closed the circle tighter, eyes glinting with hunger.

Tom looked for Daltec and Wilfred. The Wizard was sheltering in a crater as Kensa fired bolt after bolt of lightning from her staff. And the Beast Keeper was tending to Falra on the ground. Tom couldn't tell how badly hurt the Phoenix was.

*It's all going wrong… I should never have led Beasts this young into battle.*

"Tom," said Elenna, as her back pressed against his own. "I'm running out of arrows!"

Tom's shoulders burned from wielding his sword and battering with his shield, but he forced his blade up.

"We either fight our way through, or we die," said Tom.

"There are too many!" said Elenna. "Tom, if this is the end—"

"No!" said Tom. He ran at the nearest Varkule, feinting with his sword, then leaped over its head. His feet landed on its back and he jumped again to the next. He crossed the pack like stepping stones – very unsteady stepping stones – slashing with his sword to keep them at bay. Glancing back he saw that the plan had worked. The Varkules were facing him, and Elenna was safe.

Then a Varkule leaped through the air and slammed into his side, sending him sprawling onto the ground. Dizzy and gasping for air, Tom tried to stand. Another Varkule careered into his legs, upending him. Tom lost his grip on his sword and shield. He tasted blood in his mouth from biting his tongue.

The world was still spinning as he looked around. All he saw were Varkules on every side, their snarling teeth and sharp tusks ready to tear him apart. Tom's legs were weak. He had no weapons.

Tom was defeated.

# CHAPTER SIX

# THE MASK OF DEATH

A flash of blue light filled the plain
and he raised an arm to shield his
eyes.

*Raffkor!*

The young Bull Beast careered into
the midst of the Varkules. Shaking his
head from side to side, he gored and
tossed and bit. Tom saw a channel
opening up in the snarling pack.

He found his sword and shield, and managed to stagger through to safety.

The pirate ship was now at treetop level, sailing in to land. The fires on her deck were out and smoking.

Sudden anger pounded through Tom's head.

A Beast's anger.

Turning back to the Varkule pack, Tom could no longer see Raffkor at all. The Varkules were a seething mound as they fought with tusks and teeth and claws to get closer to the Bull Beast.

*He's under there somewhere*, thought Tom. *He hasn't got a chance.*

He could feel Raffkor's fury, growing by the second, like a bonfire burning out of control. Tom's body felt battered and bruised, and he could barely lift his sword, but he steeled himself.

*I can't let a Good Beast die…*

With a roar, he threw himself towards the pack.

Before he got close enough to strike, another blue light dazzled him and filled the whole plain. It crackled and flashed, and Tom was blown backwards as if by a powerful wind.

When he managed to look, he saw the mass of Varkules lying on their backs, shuddering wildly, eyes rolling back in their heads. Blue lights fizzed over their prone bodies as they squirmed. One by one, they became still and their limbs flopped lifelessly to the ground.

Only then did Tom spot Raffkor. The Bull Beast was still standing, but only just. His flanks were scarred and bleeding, rising and falling in shallow, panting breaths. His legs trembled and threatened to give way.

Worse of all, his glowing horns were pale, their blue power spent.

The sight wrenched at Tom's heart. *It's my fault...he's drained his life force to save me.*

The pain and weariness drifted from

Tom's limbs as his eyes settled on the pirate ship. *All this because Kensa wants power over Beasts.*

The rest of his companions gathered beneath the ship, bravely fighting Anoret. The faceless Beast thrashed and swiped tirelessly, and the young Beasts were falling back with Daltec and Wilfred and Elenna. Tikron trailed one broken arm and a patch of Vislak's scales had been torn away, revealing angry raw flesh beneath. Even Vedra and Krimon seemed weary, managing only small jets of fire as they struggled to stay aloft on tired wings.

The wretchedness within Tom turned slowly and darkly to anger. *I won't let it happen… Krimon! I need a hand…*

He ran at Anoret, summoning the

magic of the leg armour until he was speeding so fast the wind streamed in his hair. It felt like his feet were flying over the ground. As he reached the Beast, he sprang up her back, pushing until his thighs burned. As he reached her top spike he leaped off.

Krimon was waiting. Tom snatched at his talon and the dragon tossed him forward.

Tom sailed through the air and landed with a heavy thud on the deck of Sanpao's ship.

The pirates on deck turned as one, and hurried to draw their cutlasses. Tom's blood thundered through his veins as he leaped at them. His sword was a blur. He slashed, kicked and stabbed, scattering the pirates. One tripped over a coil of ropes, another disappeared over the deck rail with a

scream. Tom knocked a bald-headed
brute out cold with his sword hilt.

*You're no match for me!*

He broke through the ranks and
met Kensa. Her face was covered
with Anoret's blue scales, almost like

a second skin. Only her eyes and mouth were visible.

The Sorceress swirled her staff in one hand.

"No one invited you on board this ship," she said. "Do you know what we do to stowaways?"

Tom circled her. "Give up now," he said. "Give me the Mask."

"Try and take it!" she said, lunging with the staff. Tom parried with his shield and stabbed, but his blade only caught Kensa's cloak. She kicked him in the gut and he gasped in pain.

"You're supposed to protect the Beasts," she said, "but four young ones will be mine by the time the day is out. Or they will be dead!"

She brought her staff down in a vertical swipe and Tom dodged. The staff crunched into the deck, smashing the timbers.

"Not while there's blood in my veins," said Tom.

Kensa curled her lip. "So original, aren't you?"

As her shoulder twitched, Tom knew where the blow was coming.

He caught the staff with his shield. Kensa swirled, her cloak covering her attack, but again Tom seemed aware exactly where the staff would fall.

*Strange*, he thought. *It's almost like I can sense her plans before she strikes.*

Kensa's face creased into a frown. She aimed low, but Tom just knew it was a feint and held his ground.

Then he understood. *It's the Mask! It lets her communicate with Anoret, but I can sense her plans through the ruby in my belt.*

As he blocked each blow, anger flooded Kensa's eyes.

"I see you're not smiling any more," said Tom.

Her next swing was wild and out of control. Tom ducked beneath it and swiped the flat of his blade against the back of her legs. Kensa tumbled like a sack of potatoes to the deck.

Tom's hand shot to the Mask, and he tried to tug it loose. Kensa gripped his wrist and struggled to free herself, screeching madly. "No, it's mine! It's mine!"

Tom yanked as hard as he could,

but still the Mask was stuck firm.

"Let her go, bilge-rat!" bellowed Sanpao. He thundered into Tom with a shoulder-barge and Tom was lifted off the deck and crashed into the remains of the mast.

Coming to his senses, he realised he was holding something in his hand.

A tough skin of blue scales.

*The Mask!*

A hideous shrieking filled the air. Sanpao was backing away, terror painting his normally calm features. On the deck, Kensa lay on her back. Putrid black smoke rose in trails from her face. Part of Tom wanted to watch, fascinated, but another part told him to move. He sheathed his sword and in three strides he leaped over the ship's rail.

He tried to bring up his shield to

slow his fall, but he couldn't grip the handle properly while holding the Mask.

The ground rushed towards him and Tom closed his eyes, bracing himself for death.

# CHAPTER SEVEN

# THE FIRST BEAST RESTS AGAIN

Instead, he landed on something soft and warm.

When Tom dared to open his eyes, he saw white feathers, and Falra's sharp-beaked head turning back towards him. The Phoenix was missing a patch of feathers on her wing, and bleeding from her neck, but otherwise she seemed unharmed.

"Thank you!" Tom cried. Epos
would be proud of a move like that.

Falra landed among the other
Beasts, and Tom hobbled down from
her back, exhausted. The pirate ship
had turned in the sky, and voices
drifted down.

"What were you thinking?"
screamed Kensa angrily.

"I was trying to help you," Sanpao replied.

"Help me? Help me? You helped Tom take the Mask, you imbecile!"

"You're never grateful, are you? It's always the same...."

The voice of the Pirate King was lost as his ship limped off through the sky.

Tom joined his friends. All looked ready to drop, even Elenna. The Good Beasts crowded around them, bleeding and battered. And above them all, still as a statue, stood Anoret.

The faceless Beast was watching the pirate ship vanish towards the horizon. Through the ruby jewel Tom sensed nothing but confusion in her mind. "She's neither friend nor foe now."

He walked right up beneath her

huge legs, and held up the Mask.

*This belongs to you*, he said with his mind.

Anoret turned her ravaged features

towards him, then reached down with a claw. Tom tried not to flinch as the deadly scythe passed close to his head. She took the limp Mask and lifted it to her face.

He heard the others gasp as the skin and scales seemed to stretch over the exposed flesh and bone, restoring Anoret's appearance. The scars were still there, as they had been when she'd woken from the volcano, but for some reason she no longer looked so fearsome.

*She's at peace...*

"There's no anger in her now," Tom said to the others.

A message seeped into his mind.

*I am sorry, Master. And I am sorry about those young Beasts I battled today.*

"There's nothing to be sorry for," Tom replied. "Rion is safe."

Anoret turned to look above his head. *Not all of Rion.*

A strangled sob escaped Wilfred's lips, and Tom cursed himself. *How could I have forgotten Raffkor?*

He rushed alongside the Beast Keeper to where the great bull lay amid the sea of dead Varkules. Storm and Silver had rushed from the trees to his side as well. Storm neighed

softly, and Silver whined and sniffed at the motionless Bull Beast.

"He's dead," said Wilfred, falling to his knees. "I've failed and let a Good Beast perish."

Tom touched Raffkor's horn and his ruby at the same time, sadness welling in his chest.

*I'll never forget your sacrifice. You gave your life to save mine, and Rion is safe because of you.*

As soon as he'd thought the words, a booming voice responded in his head.

*There will be no sacrifice today.*

Anoret leaned over him, and reached out with a clawed foreleg. She laid it softly on the Bull Beast's flank.

With a heaving sigh, blue smoke drifted from Anoret's slitted nostrils, coiling around Raffkor's head.

"What's she doing?" asked Wilfred.

Raffkor's body twitched. Blue light flooded through his horns, and his flanks heaved in a deep breath. Tom scrambled back as the Bull Beast clambered to his feet.

"He's alive!" gasped Elenna, hugging Daltec.

Storm whinnied and Silver joined in with a howl. The other Beasts added their voices to the chorus.

Anoret turned, and began to walk away.

"Wait!" called Tom. "Where are you going?"

Anoret stopped and looked at them all. Through the ruby, Tom felt a flood of affection.

*My time here is over. Stonewin calls me back to my resting place. These brave*

*Beasts are the future now. The kingdoms
are theirs to guard. And you will watch
over them.* Her gaze fell on Tom. *Tanner
would be proud of you, Tom of Errinel.*

Anoret continued on her way,
her slow strides making the ground
shake.

Tom's heart felt close to bursting as
he watched the Beast leave.

"Are you all right?" asked Elenna.

Tom realised his friend was smiling at him. She couldn't have heard the words Anoret was speaking, but she must have understood a little.

"Everything is fine," he said.

Around them, the young Beasts gathered closer, each standing tall and proud. Falra ruffled her snowy feathers and the twin dragons blasted two jets of flame that crossed in the sky. Raffkor gave Wilfred a playful shove with his snout that almost knocked the Beast Keeper over. Luckily, Vislak caught him in a coil and set him upright again. Tikron gave a series of howling cries which might have been laughter.

*They're still young now*, thought Tom, *but they proved themselves today.*

"Ready to go home?" asked Daltec.

"I think I'd rather ride," said Elenna with a smile. "You might magic us into the palace moat by accident."

Daltec's face fell.

"I'm only teasing," said Elenna. "Let's go."

"I hope to see you again soon," said Wilfred.

"And under better circumstances," said Tom. "Keep these young Beasts safe. Our future may depend on them."

"I will," said Wilfred. "Farewell."

Daltec muttered a spell under his breath, and the fields of Rion vanished before Tom's eyes.

*Back to Avantia*, he thought. *Until Evil strikes again.*

Tom's Quest continues in a
brand new series,
THE CURSED DRAGON.
Coming soon!

## Series 13: THE WARRIOR'S ROAD
## COLLECT THEM ALL!

The Warrior's Road is Tom's toughest challenge
yet. Will he succeed where so many have failed?

978 1 40832 402 8

978 1 40832 403 5

978 1 40832 404 2

978 1 40832 405 9

978 1 40832 406 6

978 1 40832 407 3

# Win an exclusive
# Beast Quest T-shirt and goody bag!

In every Beast Quest book the Beast Quest logo is
hidden in one of the pictures. Find the logo in this book
and make a note of which page it appears on.
Write the page number on a postcard and
send it in to us.
Each month we will draw one winner to receive
a Beast Quest T-shirt and goody bag.

THE BEAST QUEST COMPETITION:
ANORET THE FIRST BEAST
Orchard Books
338 Euston Road, London NW1 3BH
Australian readers should email:
childrens.books@hachette.com.au

New Zealand readers should write to:
Beast Quest Competition
4 Whetu Place, Mairangi Bay, Auckland, NZ
or email: childrensbooks@hachette.co.nz

Only one entry per child.
Closing date: 31 January 2014

You can also enter this competition
via the Beast Quest website: www.beastquest.co.uk

## Fight the Beasts,
## Fear the Magic

# www.beastquest.co.uk

Have you checked out the Beast Quest website?
It's the place to go for games, downloads, activities,
sneak previews and lots of fun!

You can read all about your favourite beasts, download free screensavers and desktop wallpapers for your computer, and even challenge your friends to a Beast Tournament.

Sign up to the newsletter at www.beastquest.co.uk to receive exclusive extra content and the opportunity to enter special members-only competitions. We'll send you up-to-date info on all the Beast Quest books, including the next exciting series which features four brand-new Beasts!

FREE COLLECTOR CARDS INSIDE!

≫ **Series 1** ≪

# COLLECT THEM ALL!

Have you read all the books in Series 1 of
BEAST QUEST? Read on to find out where
it all began in this sneak peek from book 1,
FERNO THE FIRE DRAGON...

978 1 84616 483 5

978 1 84616 482 8

978 1 84616 484 2

978 1 84616 486 6

978 1 84616 485 9

978 1 84616 487 3

# CHAPTER ONE

# THE
# MYSTERIOUS FIRE

Tom stared hard at his enemy.
"Surrender, villain!" he cried. "Surrender,
or taste my blade!"

He gave the sack of hay a firm blow
with the poker. "That's you taken care
of," he announced. "One day I'll be
the finest swordsman in all of Avantia.
Even better than my father, Taladon the
Swift!"

Tom felt the ache in his heart that
always came when he thought about
his father. The uncle and aunt who had
brought Tom up since he was a baby
never spoke about him or why he had
left Tom to their care after Tom's mother
had died.

He shoved the poker back into its pack. "One day I'll know the truth," he swore.

As Tom walked back to the village, a sharp smell caught at the back of his throat.

"Smoke!" he thought.

He stopped and looked around. Through the trees to his left, he could hear a faint crackling as a wave of warm air hit him.

*Fire!*

Tom pushed his way through the trees and burst into a field. The golden wheat had been burned to black stubble and a veil of smoke hung in the air. Tom stared in horror. How had this happened?

He looked up and blinked. For a second he thought he saw a dark shape moving towards the hills in the distance. But then the sky was empty again.

An angry voice called out. "Who's there?"